LADY OF THE LOOKING GLASS

A SHORT STORY

ALEXANDRIA BLAELOCK

BlueMere Books
MELBOURNE, AUSTRALIA

For permission requests, please contact
enquiries@bluemerebooks.com.

Ordering Information:
Discounts are available on quantity purchases. For details, contact orders@bluemerebooks.com.

Lady of the Looking Glass/Alexandria Blaelock
paperback ISBN: 978-1-925749-13-7
digital ISBN: 978-1-925749-12-0

Book Layout © BookDesignTemplates.com

LADY OF THE
LOOKING GLASS

Jessica woke feeling hot and sweaty with a thumping headache.

Not entirely unexpected when you're in your twenties after a long night clubbing.

Even when you're not drinking.

The room smelled stale and overcooked, as if the curtains had been open and the windows closed on a midsummer day.

She rubbed her dry and gritty eyes, and thought her skin felt strangely dry and loose.

She sat up too quickly, and as the dizziness hit, fell back down.

After a moment, she rolled on her back, opened her eyes and looked up at a blurry ceiling she didn't recognise.

Not moving her head, she tentatively reached out with both hands, encountering only empty space.

Her eyes teared up, and she closed them in relief.

Firstly, she was probably alone, and secondly, after the initial sting, her eyes felt so much better.

She opened them again, and as gently as possible, moved her head from side to side to see what was there.

She relaxed slightly as she realised she was alone, but tensed again almost immediately as she became aware she was naked in a room she didn't recognise.

And needed to pee badly.

Pulling a sheet around her, she slid off the bed and stood unsteadily.

Great. Now she wanted to puke too.

Hoping the door she was facing was a bathroom, she half ran, half fell and pushed it open.

Sliding to her knees in front of the toilet she vomited until she was left dry retching.

Utterly spent, she allowed herself to collapse on the cold tiled floor.

Coming to sometime later, she lay still, eyes closed, and tried to remember where she was, and why.

She'd gone out with the girls for Sarah's hen night. There'd been a party bus taking them from club to club.

As Maid of Honour, she'd been limiting her drinks so she could make sure no one was hurt or forgotten.

They'd gone into some bar with a loud techno beat. There'd been dancing. There'd been shouting.

She'd seen a beautiful boy with mesmerising blue eyes.

And that was about it.

This wasn't her home, so logically, it was his.

Had he given her some kind of drug? Was it him though, or someone else?

She still needed to pee.

Leaning on the wall, she gently stood up, and flushed the vomit filled toilet. After waving her hands to freshen the air, she sat to pee.

The bathroom smelled somewhat comfortingly of steam and cologne.

It was luxuriously full of black marble and chrome fittings, with soft thick red towels layered haphazardly on the rails.

Not exactly to her taste, but nice enough.

If not for the messy pile of well-worn slippers, smear of toothpaste on the vanity, and half full skin care containers, it almost looked like a hotel or design magazine bathroom.

It certainly didn't look like a young man's bathroom.

Though when you're renting, you pretty much go with whatever's there don't you?

Or did he live at home with his parents?

Mind you, if he'd used the room this morning, it could still be a hotel.

If it was him.

There was nothing to suggest who it might've been.

Jessica massaged her temples where the headache was threatening to return.

Cleaning up and flushing the toilet again, she approached the vanity to wash up.

The woman in the venetian glass mirror was old. Not like really old, but old enough to be her mother.

She splashed her face with cold water, and rubbed her eyes.

The woman's greying hair was in a neat longish bob, or at least it would probably be neat when it was combed out.

Her face and crepey chest harboured the odd age spot. The face wasn't that bad for an old chick - judging by the number of pots of lotion on the bathroom counter she worked hard to maintain it.

With her slightly full cheeks, and lightly padded body, she looked like a comfortable middle-aged housewife.

Not that there's anything wrong with middle aged housewives.

She waved, and the housewife waved back.

Freaky.

She waved again, then shuffled to the right and back. The woman in the mirror did the same.

She tried a few random lunges and the woman kept up.

It was impossible, yet it seemed that somehow, she and the woman in the mirror were the same person.

Where was the woman who owned this body if she was here instead?

How was it possible that last night she was dancing with a beautiful boy, and this morning she was in this old body, in this luxuriously tawdry bathroom?

Was she still Jessica, or was she someone else?

Had she travelled in time or was there something wrong with her brain?

Maybe she was hallucinating?

Yes, that was her best hope.

Hallucinating for sure.

Closing her eyes, she prodded her face hopefully, and felt the pressure.

Not reassured, she pinched her neck hard enough to hurt.

And opened her eyes in surprise.

The old woman was still there. Scowling at her.

Closing her eyes again, she bent and leant her head on the cool marble vanity.

Okay.

So.

However she came to be here, this was the body she was in. And she felt a little embarrassed about the saggy arms and baggy legs.

Was that what middle aged bodies looked like? She'd never seen one.

And if she was here in this body, where was its owner? Was she cavorting around town in Jessica's body *Freaky Friday* style?

For a moment she was filled with terror, but reassured herself that a middle-aged woman was unlikely to run amok in her body.

Was she?

Something had to be done, but what?

First a hot shower, some clean clothes and then buckets of strong coffee.

And then maybe she could think.

She locked the bathroom door, and took the quickest possible shower.

Partly because she didn't want to touch the body, and partly because she was afraid someone would try to open the door.

While towelling herself dry, she reviewed the pots on the vanity, then smeared on some face cream, spritzed herself with Chanel No 5 and combed her hair.

The body's hair?

Next step, find some clothes.

Leaving the wet towels on the floor, she wrapped herself in a dry one and returned to the bedroom where she was confronted by enormous photos of the old woman on the walls.

Aside from shuddering, she didn't know how to deal with that.

What kind of person hangs larger than life photos of themselves in their bedroom?

How confident did you have to be to choose that size over a standard 5" x 7"?

They looked professional; was this woman a model or actor?

Opposite the bed, was a black and white portrait at a beach tide line. Her jeans were rolled up, sandals dangling from her left hand while the right held down her stripy t-shirt. The wind was whipping her hair, and her head was thrown back laughing.

For a photo taken in a public setting, it was surprisingly intimate, she wasn't pretending to be something she wasn't. She'd let her guard down, and was just being who she was at that moment.

For an instant Jessica could almost remember the moment the picture was taken; her comfort with her body, not feeling the need to conform with the expectations of others, the joy of living the life she was living.

Above the bed there was a colour image; wearing a plain black slip or dress, seated on a chair. Her elbow resting on crossed knee, she was leaning forward and looking out into the room, one shoestring strap slipping down her shoulder.

Jessica shuffled sideways, but freakily, it seemed the woman's eyes followed her.

She looked sexually confident, bold and confronting, as if she was assessing Jessica's abilities and trying to decide whether to invite her into bed.

Jessica couldn't quite resolve the difference between the appearance of this brazen woman with the one she'd seen in the mirror.

Was the difference that she was inside the body, not its owner?

Would another twenty years of life give her the confidence to take up space, or was there something about the woman that marked her apart from "normal" women.

Shaking her head, she opened another door.

At first, she thought she'd blundered into a shop, but it was "just" a dressing room.

One wall was lined with large mirrors that reflected rails of elegant skirts, blouses and dresses hanging on the opposite.

There were shelves of bags and shoes, and racks of jewellery, glasses and belts.

The clothing was simple and elegant in vibrant pure toned colours.

Whoever this woman was, she had overwhelmingly exquisite taste.

Ignoring the menswear, Jessica walked along the racks touching garments here and there.

The fabrics were rich and lush, and while the shapes weren't body con, they were more closely fitted than the jeans and loose t-shirts she normally wore.

It was a grown up's wardrobe, specifically, that bold woman's.

She opened a few drawers at random and found soft knits, beautiful matching lace underwear and jeans.

All carefully folded and laid in the drawers.

Reminding herself she could be interrupted any moment, she quickly threw on jeans and after hesitating at a pile of striped t-shirts, picked a plain red one.

Then she tried on a couple of pairs of glasses, which fixed the blurriness, and went with a plain black frame.

Despite the body owning the clothes, she felt like a thief as she returned to the bedroom.

The last door led into a corridor, and following it to the end, she found herself in a sleek minimalist kitchen.

The first thing she saw was an empty cup on the bench surrounded by a sprinkle of sugar.

Noting the fragrance of coffee mixed with cologne, she froze and listened carefully, but was reassured by the sound of silence.

The second thing she saw was the espresso maker, and seemingly its usual owner was not at her best in the morning as everything Jessica needed was right next to it.

With coffee on the go, and the cold, empty cup in the sink, she paid more attention to the room.

It was a large open plan living dining room with the kitchen taking up one end.

The outer wall was made of glass, looking out over a wooden deck into a lush garden.

The space was almost ready for a magazine photo shoot.

It was minimally decorated with a couple of large abstract paintings.

The old wooden furniture was plain and practical, the cushions and area rugs pulled colours from the paintings.

The flat surfaces were clear, and what she had originally taken to be wooden walls were actually built in cupboards concealing entertainment appliances.

Despite its sparseness, it felt comfortable and relaxed.

She could imagine herself living in this space. Almost see herself and the beautiful boy sharing this space with a big hairy dog.

Happily ever after if you will.

By now she was intrigued by the bold woman who owned this body.

Who was she?

What did she do?

How did she come to live in this house?

Who did she share it with?

She finished making the coffee, and taking the cup with her, tracked back along the corridor.

Two plain but serviceable bedrooms, neither showing any signs of recent use or ownership.

A similarly plain and serviceable family bathroom, and a laundry room.

A messy room full of pieces of computers and stacks of boxes of wires and other weird man stuff.

Opening the last door, she found herself in a sparse modernist study.

Three walls were clad with floor to ceiling bookshelves stuffed with books. In the fourth,

French doors opened into a smallish Mediterranean style courtyard.

Nearby a black Le Corbusier style recliner sat under a floor lamp, next to a coffee table with an empty cup and upside down book propped on it.

A slim wooden desk was topped with a silver photo frame, a thin closed laptop, a notebook decorated with a couple of post-it notes and bookmarked with a red fountain pen. Lastly, a small glass milk bottle containing a single red rose.

Jessica sat on a black Eames replica chair at the desk and picked up the photo. It showed the old woman with a distinguished grey-haired man who looked vaguely familiar.

They were wearing formal attire, he wore a black tuxedo, and her a long elegant cobalt blue gown.

They looked happy, standing side by side, arms linked, leaning slightly towards each other. At ease with each other; clearly a very intimate relationship.

Sitting in the woman's body, in her chair, at her desk, in her home, Jessica was suddenly violently jealous.

She had no idea how she came to be in the body, but she didn't want to give it back.

This woman seemed to have everything she wanted - confidence, a man who loved her, and a beautiful home.

She took up space, you couldn't ignore her, or brush her under the carpet.

But she'd just woken up in the body with no idea how she got there, let alone how to stay there.

She couldn't think.

She needed more coffee to work it through.

Taking both empty cups back to the kitchen, she was bending to rinse hers in the sink when she overbalanced and hit her head on an overhead cabinet, knocking herself out and falling to the floor.

《《 • 》》

Jessica woke feeling hot and sweaty with a thumping headache. She was surprised to find herself in a bed, and not on the floor.

Reaching up to her head, she was shocked for a moment to discover her hair was short, until she remembered she wore her hair in a short pixie, not a long bob.

When she opened her eyes, she saw the stained ceiling in horrifyingly clear detail.

Concerned she didn't recognise the room. And that someone else was in the bed with her.

Not that it mattered, she was going to be sick.

Disregarding her nakedness, she half ran and half fell through the door she was facing into a bathroom.

Sliding to her knees in front of the toilet, she vomited until there was nothing left.

Willing herself not to pass out, she stood slowly, flushed the toilet and walked to the vanity.

The face in the mirror was her own, which on the one hand was reassuring, but on the other, there was that grown-up life she'd been on the verge of embracing.

A male voice called out from the bedroom, "are you okay in there?"

Jessica smiled wryly at herself in the mirror, that sounded like the beautiful boy.

"Nothing a cup of coffee won't cure."

"I've only got instant; will that be ok?"

"I think it will be better than nothing – though you'd better make it two spoons."

He snorted, and she heard him walking away.

She splashed water on her face to freshen herself up.

Thankfully, the towel smelled clean so she dried her face on it and returned to the bedroom.

The sparsely furnished, reasonably clean and tidy bachelor's room.

As she started looking for her clothes, she could hear him opening cupboards and rattling stuff in the kitchen.

Was he giving her time to get dressed?

How sweet.

She found her clothes but couldn't help comparing them with the beautiful ones in the old lady's wardrobe.

Jessica sat on the bed to dress and wondered what the old woman would do in her situation.

Unlikely she'd wake up in some random bloke's house, but if she did, she'd probably be prepared with fresh lipstick and maybe some clean clothes.

She probably wouldn't feel embarrassed or apologise, nor would she make excuses and rush out of the place.

She'd drink her coffee, chat a bit, and make a decision about whether a relationship with beautiful boy had any promise.

And whatever she chose, she'd move ahead with confidence in herself.

Jessica grinned.

She'd stroll nonchalantly into the kitchen in her short sparkly dress and bare feet, try to hold a grown-up conversation with him while she drank her instant coffee.

And if he looked as promising this morning as she remembered from last night, she'd order him an espresso maker when she got home.

Then she'd start thinking about how she could become the kind of person who hung larger than life photos of herself on her bedroom walls.

THE END

ABOUT THE AUTHOR

Alexandria Blaelock writes stories, some of them for *Ellery Queen's Mystery Magazine* and *Pulphouse Fiction Magazine*. She's also written four self-help books applying business techniques to personal matters like getting dressed, cleaning house, and feeding your friends.

As a recovering Project Manager, she's probably too fond of sticking to plan. She lives in a forest because she enjoys birdsong, the scent of gum leaves and the sun on her face. When not telecommuting to parallel universes from her Melbourne based imagination, she watches K-dramas, talks to animals, and drinks Campari. At the same time.

Discover more at www.alexandriablaelock.com.

BOOKS BY
ALEXANDRIA BLAELOCK

Stress Free Dinner Parties
Build Your Signature Wardrobe
Holistic Personal Finance
Ms Blaelock's Book of Minimally Viable
Housekeeping

www.ingramcontent.com/pod-product-compliance
Lightning Source LLC
Chambersburg PA
CBHW070456170726
48291CB00005B/1773